Published by Ladybird Books Ltd
A Penguin Company
Penguin Books Ltd, 80 Strand, London WC2R 0RL, England
Penguin Books Australia Ltd, 250 Camberwell Road, Camberwell, Victoria 3124, Australia
Penguin Books (NZ) Ltd, Cnr Rosedale and Airborne Roads, Albany, Auckland, New Zealand

Meg and Mog Television Series copyright © Absolutely/Happy Life/Varga 2003
Based upon the books featuring the characters Meg and Mog
by Helen Nicoll and Jan Pieńkowski
Licensed by Target Entertainment
This book based on the TV episode **Meg's Cauldron**
Script by Carl Gorham and Moray Hunter
Animation artwork by Roger Mainwood
First published by Ladybird Books 2004
4 6 8 10 9 7 5
Copyright © Absolutely/Happy Life/Varga, 2004
Printed in Italy

MEG & MOG

Meg's Cauldron

created by
Helen Nicoll and Jan Pieńkowski

Meg's cauldron was a hundred years old.

"It's the cauldron's birthday today," said Meg. "I'll do a spell for a birthday cake."

"Ear of toad
   and tongue of snake,
   Make a special
   birthday cake!"

Meg and Owl stood well back.

But where was the usual lightning bolt and thunder clap? The cauldron let out a small puff of smoke and was silent. Something was very wrong.

They took the cauldron to the workshop.

"Can you mend it for us?" Meg asked the mechanic.

"Well, I'll do my best," he said,
shaking his head. "But in the
meantime why don't you borrow
this? It's the latest model."

And he produced a shining, brand
new cauldron with all sorts of
interesting knobs and dials.

"Wow!" said Meg, Mog and Owl.

They took the new cauldron
home and put it in the kitchen.
Meg pressed the starter button.
A high-pitched voice said:

"NAME YOUR SPELL. NAME YOUR
SPELL."

"A talking cauldron!" said Meg.

"I CAN DO ANYTHING," said the cauldron. "NAME YOUR SPELL."

"We'll let you know as soon as we need you," said Meg. "We're just going to have tea."

The cauldron whirred and flickered and a tremendous flash of light filled the kitchen.

When it died down, the table had been laid with a delicious meal. "TEA IS SERVED," said the cauldron.

"That was nice and quick," said Meg, as they sat down to eat. "At this rate it won't be long before bedtime."

"BEDTIME . . .
BEDTIME . . ."
said the cauldron.

There was another flash of light and suddenly the bed had appeared in the kitchen. Meg, Mog and Owl found themselves tucked up in it.

"But we haven't had our tea yet,"
said Owl.

"And we don't sleep in the kitchen,"
said Meg.

"NOT IN THE KITCHEN . . ." said the cauldron, and with another flash, the bed and all its occupants were out in the garden.

"We don't sleep in the garden either," said Meg crossly.

"NOT IN THE GARDEN . . ." said the cauldron.

Flash! The bed flew up to the top of the house and balanced on the chimney.

"And we certainly don't sleep on the roof," said Meg.

"These are some of the worst spells I've ever seen," said Mog.

"And that's saying something," muttered Owl.

Meg ignored him. They were all wishing they had their old cauldron back.

After an uncomfortable night on the roof, Meg was pleased to see the mechanic at the door the next morning. But he was very gloomy.

He handed Meg a sack. "I'm afraid I've tried everything with your cauldron, but its days are over."

The cauldron was in pieces.

Meg, Mog and Owl stood around
the remains of their old friend,
feeling very sad. The new
cauldron came up
and nudged them.

"NAME YOUR SPELL. NAME YOUR
SPELL. COME ON. KEEP ME BUSY.
I CAN DO ANYTHING."

"Oh, be quiet!" said Meg. "I'm sorry,
but our poor old cauldron is broken
and useless. We'll never get it back."

The new cauldron bounced up and down. "WHY DIDN'T YOU SAY? I CAN DO ANYTHING."

And with the biggest flash of all, the new cauldron vanished and there in the middle of the kitchen floor was the old cauldron, looking exactly as it had always done.

"It's back!" cried Meg.

"How are you, old cauldron?" asked Owl.

"There's only one way to find out," said Meg. "I'll do a spell."

**"Ear of toad
and tongue of snake,
Make a special
birthday cake!"**

The old cauldron let off a
terrific bolt of lightning and
a clap of thunder, and a
birthday cake shot out of
its mouth.

The cake
exploded on
the ceiling.
Cake crumbs
scattered
everywhere
and a lot
of the
icing
landed
on Meg's
head.

The old cauldron was definitely
back.

"Happy birthday, old cauldron!" said
Meg.